WE WERE MADE FOR EACH OTHER!

Text and Illustrations by Jiu Er
Read by Julie Nesrallah

My name is
Little Sun.
I'm a rather
quiet pig.
I like to share my
favourite things!
I make friends
easily.
And I'm always on the
lookout for challenges
big or small.

I have lots
of friends.

Sometimes
I feel lonely.

I like to dream and
mull things over.

I love to draw!

And capture each moment
in a new picture!

Like everyone, I suppose,
every now and then
I would like to be different
or look like someone else,
just as someone else
might want to be like me.
We have all met someone
along the way who inspires us.

Sometimes we meet people
at exactly the right moment!
Just as I was hoping to trade
my basket of carrots for a tasty watermelon,
Miss Rabbit was thinking
that she would like to trade her watermelon
for a basket of tasty carrots.

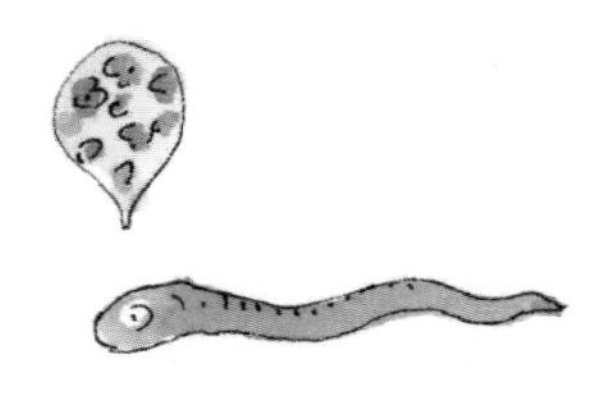

Trust me, my dear Little Mouse.
Don't be sad that you're so small—
our dreams are always bigger
than we are!

Dear Little Mouse, don't forget
to plant these seeds
when you are happy.
That way, they'll grow
into beautiful flowers!
Then when people see them,
they too will be filled with joy.
So...are you ready?

Don't be sad, Little Mouse—
that's just how life is.
Often you have to start over many times
before you find the right path.

Along life's way,
sometimes we have to take a chance,
don't we? I'm not afraid!
We have to trust our friends,
who can help us
overcome our fears!

In our dreams, we fly over oceans.
It's beautiful to soar like that—
I can't imagine anything more beautiful.
But sometimes in a dream
you can fly all night
without ever finding a single place to land.
So the only thing to do is keep on flying,
no matter how tired or frightened you become.
Luckily, you always wake up in the end.
Back on solid ground,
the journey seems to have been so much easier!

At the park, we were stuck sitting
in the same position
for at least an hour.
I couldn't go up
and Little Mouse couldn't come down.
Each as stubborn as the other,
we stayed that way without moving.

A good book can cure heartache
but it can't always heal
scratches and bruises.

My dear Little Mouse,
remember on fine afternoons
to hang your bedspread outdoors!
That way, when night comes,
you'll still be able to smell
the sunshine!

My, how difficult it was
to convince Little Mouse
that there's nothing better
than taking a good bath!
What's worse, right in the middle
the water stopped running
and there she was with her eyes
full of soap bubbles!
But instead of complaining,
she wisely said, "The water will eventually
come back on. There's no problem.
We just need to wait for a while,
just a short while..."

Even the strongest,
toughest people can be sad.
Unfortunately, I can't stop the pain,
but I will always be there
to help you get through.

The movie was so much fun
and the popcorn delicious!
My dear Little Mouse,
we need to learn to enjoy
every moment of happiness.
It will help us face
life's little worries with confidence.

The truth is that
when you experience
a moment of happiness,
it may be because someone
has done something nice
without telling you
or wanting you to know.

During a long journey,
we may not all see the same scenery.
"Is there still grass over there?"
asked Little Mouse.
"No," I explained,
"there are also bushes and fruit trees!"
"Exactly! And further still,
a magnificent lake," added Giraffe.

Sport

From my point of view,
the decision may be an easy one:
to hang on or let go?
For Little Mouse, however,
things are much more complicated
and the consequences more serious.

Day after day, year after year,
time changes many things.
Yet I have only to look in the mirror
to see the reflection of that
which is most precious to me.

Some situations
always warm the heart.

遇见

Far from home,
Miss Rabbit is homesick.
Having a good cry
helps her feel better.
It sometimes takes
more courage to admit
your weakness
than it does to pretend
to be strong.

I wanted to prepare
some big, tasty dumplings.
Little Mouse prefers ravioli.
“To each his own,” she said.
“I agree!” was my answer.
Together, batch by batch,
first one then the other,
we made dumplings
and ravioli.

Sometimes it's so hard
to find inspiration!
Little Mouse had an idea:
"If you really don't know what to draw,
Little Sun, why don't you come down
and play for a while?
Whenever we play together,
you always come up
with lots of great ideas!"

紧急制动
中国

Mrs. Cow, who is sitting
across from Little Mouse
and myself, enjoys sad stories
more than anything else.
They always touch
her very deeply.
Without making a sound,
I offer her a tissue.
Sometimes we learn more
from sorrow
than from happiness.

Nothing to brag about—
I haven't done
anything exceptional.
I simply borrowed
some beauty from
these lovely flowers.

Growing tall and strong requires practice.

Little Mouse is getting down to work.

I have to admit that my hearty laughter is a bit much! That's because I don't want to hurt Little Mouse's feelings.
I read this book of jokes a long time ago and know them all by heart.

Miss Rabbit isn't fooled,
but she doesn't say a word.

Miss Rabbit and I came to keep Little Mouse company as she waited for a shooting star to pass overhead.
She reminded us to make a wish just as the star crosses the sky.
But when we finally did see a shooting star, Little Mouse was fast asleep, her little paws clenched. My wish?
That Little Mouse's wish comes true!

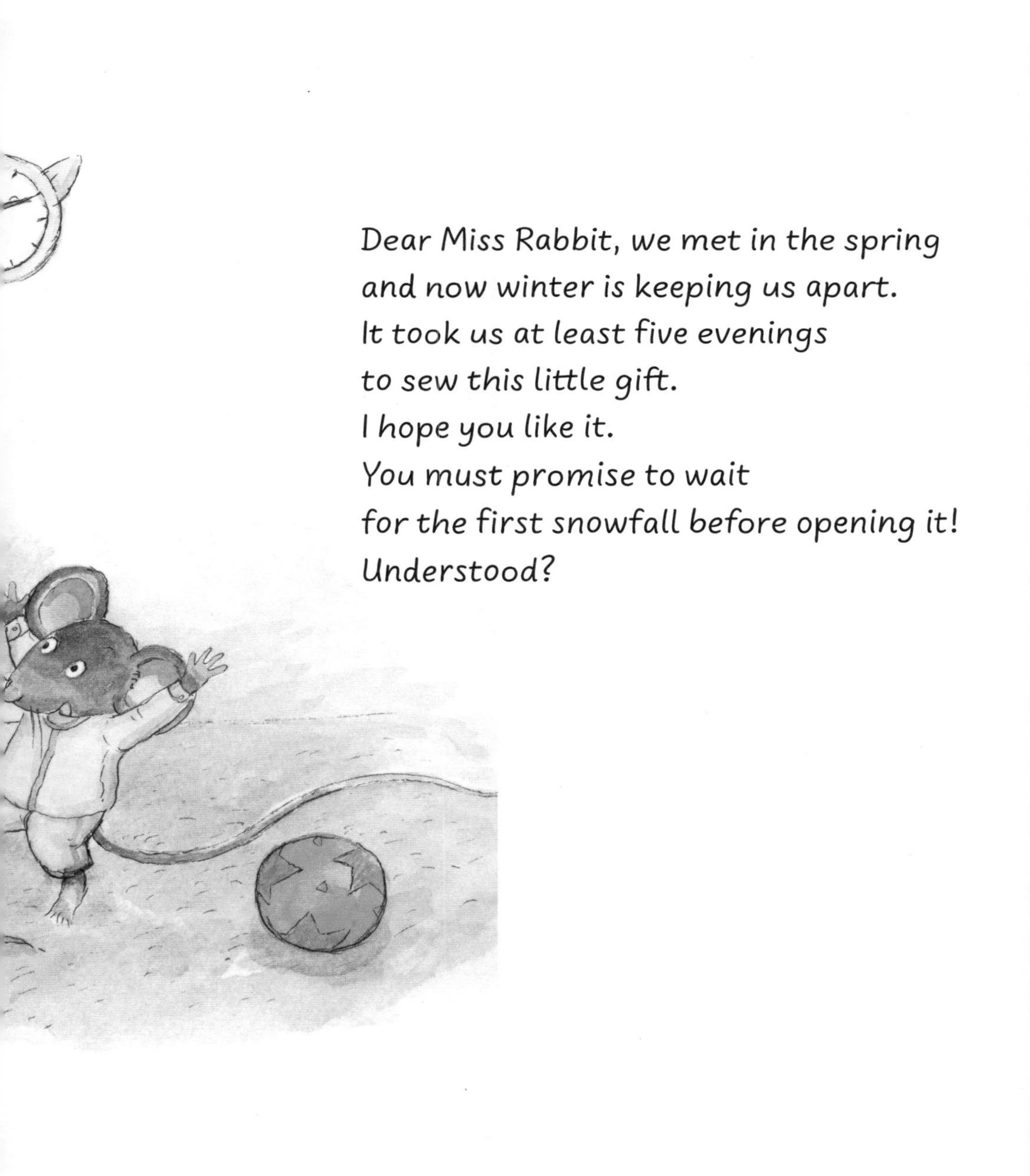

Dear Miss Rabbit, we met in the spring
and now winter is keeping us apart.
It took us at least five evenings
to sew this little gift.
I hope you like it.
You must promise to wait
for the first snowfall before opening it!
Understood?

小猪修复店

I started a repair business,
and it has been very successful.
However, there is something
I don't understand.
Why is it that so many toys
need to be fixed?
With great care, I put them back together
until they're just like new!

An artist by the name of Jiu Er
came to see me. She was very sad.
She asked me if I also knew
how to fix a broken heart.
I looked into her tear-filled eyes.
It's so hard to not be able
to heal someone's pain.

小猪修复店
妹妹的大南瓜

Life is also about asking questions
and wondering about things.
But there's no doubt
that the more you question,
the harder it is to see clearly!

We have tried to fly many times
but never succeeded.
Each time, we fell quickly back
to the foot of the mountain.
So we decided to climb it instead.
When we finally reached the top,
we found an angel sitting there
sad and wistful.
He told us that he was tired
from the weight of such heavy wings
and that he no longer cared to fly...

As I went on my way,
I came upon
a magnificent field
with hundreds
of flowers blooming.
Rather than picking them,
I gathered some seeds
to keep as a precious treasure.
Later, I will offer them
to Little Mouse,
whom I have not seen
for some time.

Don't be sad, dear Little Mouse.
When you need me most,
I will always be there for you.
That's what friends are for!

We first met five years,
four months and sixteen days ago.
To celebrate this important anniversary,
we baked some small cakes
to remind us how fine life is
and to remember to enjoy all it has to offer.
Little Sun and Little Mouse are truly
the best friends in the world!

Dear Little Mouse,
must you really sit there,
lost in your thoughts?
Let me give this plant some water
before it loses all its leaves.

Dear Little Mouse,
life can sometimes be drab,
so our dreams should always be colourful.
I imagined this car.
I hope that one day you and I
will take a trip in it.
Wouldn't that just be so much fun?

Do you know what, dear Little Mouse?
Working hard always makes you feel
you've learned more.

This little creature
who makes it thunder and rain
may be a little monster,
but she is still afraid of her own noise.
Boom! Boom! Boom!
With every clap of thunder,
her heart jumps!

Getting together with friends
is always such a happy occasion.
No matter whether the road is bumpy
or covered in mud,
as long as we are together,
nothing can daunt us!

In the middle of a snowy forest
on the coldest day of winter,
seeing you always warms my heart.

Reading is a wonderful thing,
for it allows us to escape into
completely different worlds.
Right now, for example,
even though we are sitting side
by side, we are all far away
in the stories we are reading!

妖怪山

My friend Monster Frog
has many small eyes on her head
and can therefore boast of seeing
in all directions at once.
That doesn't make her any happier, though,
because when you can see
in every direction, anywhere,
every which way,
knowing which way to go
is that much harder.
She always ends up lost!

My diary,
signed Little Sun.

Every time I leave home,
my mother reminds me to be careful.
A good little pig like me
wouldn't hurt a fly.
What my mother forgets, though,
is that there are many others in this world
whose lives are far more fragile
than that of a little pig,
and we need to look after them.
All those other lives are important
and full of dreams
just waiting to come true.

As time goes by, I am ever more convinced
that my appearance has nothing to do
with the good food I eat.
It's merely a coincidence!

Although I've made many masks
to please others,
my favourite is still my own:
that of an adorable little pig.

Pretty little fish, how I do love you!
Pretty little fish, I am going
to look after you so well!
Only, sometimes, accidents can happen
precisely because we try so hard
to avoid them!

Please don't look at me
as though I were perfect,
and don't worry about me, either...really!
I am very aware of how lucky I am
to have everything I have,
and I appreciate it.
Remember: I'm Little Sun, the tiny pig!

Being small must make him so sad!
完美手册

Artists are the most generous people I know.
They donate colourful drawings
to blank pages!

Even the most hideous monsters
sometimes find themselves in a knot
with all their little problems.
Like the hairs on our head,
our little joys and troubles always come and go
and sometimes get all mixed up.
There's a simple solution, though:
just buy a small bowtie,
make two braids at the back of your head
and presto!—
all your problems are straightened out
and you're good to go!

Can I give you a hug? After all,
we were made for each other!

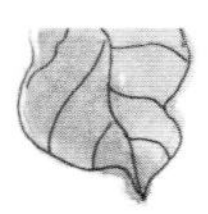

西藏生死书

Text and Illustrations by Jiu Er Read by Julie Nesrallah
Sound Designer, Composer and Record Producer Olaf Gundel
Artistic Director Roland Stringer
Graphic Design Stephan Lorti pour Haus Design
Translation Alexandre Zouaghi and Helen Roulston
for Services d'édition Guy Connolly

First published in Chinese by Beijing Dandelion Children's Publishing House Co., Ltd.
in 2015 under the title The Perfect Encounter (想要最好的遇) by Jiu Er (九儿).

The audio recording can be listened to for free on The Secret Mountain website
at www.thesecretmountain.com/portfolio/we-were-made-for-each-other.
It contains contains the sound of a musical instrument as a signal for
the young reader to turn the page.

www.thesecretmountain.com

ISBN 13: 978-2-924774-22-9 / ISBN 10: 2-924217-22-5

Printed in Hong Kong by Book Art Inc. (Toronto)